What was the alligator's
favorite game?

Snap!

Why did the orange fall asleep at work?

He ran out of juice!

How do owls send messages
around the forest?

By tree mail!

Ridiculous
Q & A Jokes!

Why did the tiger spit out the clown?
He tasted funny!

Why did the fish live in salt water?
Pepper made him sneeze!

What is a good gift for
a baby ghost?
Boootees!

THE BEST JOKES FOR

6

YEAR OLD KIDS!

OVER 250 FUNNY JOKES!

With over 250 really funny,
hilarious Jokes,
The Best Jokes For 6 Year Old Kids!
promises hours of fun for
the whole family!

Includes brand new, original and
classic Jokes that will have the kids
(and adults!) in fits of laughter
in no time!

These jokes are so funny it's going
to be hard not to laugh!
Just wait until you hear the
giggles and laughter!

Books by Freddy Frost

The Best Jokes For 6 Year Old Kids
The Best Jokes For 7 Year Old Kids
The Best Jokes For 8 Year Old Kids
The Best Jokes For 9 Year Old Kids
The Best Jokes For 10 Year Old Kids
The Best Jokes For 11 Year Old Kids
The Best Jokes For 12 Year Old Kids

To see all the latest books by Freddy Frost just go to
FreddyFrost.com

Contents

Funny Q & A Jokes! 5

Funnier Knock Knock Jokes! 18

Laugh Out Loud Q & A Jokes! 31

Crazy Knock Knock Jokes!...........44

Ridiculous Q & A Jokes! 57

Silly Knock Knock Jokes!.............70

Bonus Q & A Jokes! 83

Bonus Knock Knock Jokes! 96

Thank you! 108

Funny Q & A Jokes!

Why didn't the teddy wear
shoes to school?
He liked to have bear feet!

What do you call a snowman
on a hot day?
Puddle!

How does a bee get to work?
He waits at the buzz stop!

What do cats put in their drinks?
Mice Cubes!

What shoes do mice wear?
Squeakers!

What did the cloud wear
underneath his raincoat?
Thunderpants!

Why did the girl take her
ruler to bed?
To see how long she slept!

Why don't elephants get paid much?
They work for peanuts!

How did the fish get to work?
He hailed a crab!

What game do mice play?
Hide and squeak!

What do elves love learning the most
at school?
The elf-abet!

What do you call a football playing cat?
Puss in boots!

What did the big cow say to
the small cow?

Mooooooove over!

Why did the cat jump up
on the computer?

So she could catch the mouse!

Why did the puppy sit in the sun?

He wanted to be a hot dog!

What did the egg in a hurry
say to the other egg?
Let's get cracking!

What did the leopard say after lunch?
That really hit the spots!

What is Santa's dog called?
Santa Paws!

Why did the pony stop
singing in the farm band?
She was a little hoarse!

What kind of tie does a boy pig wear?
A pigsty!

What did the hedgehog
say to the cactus?
Hi dad!

What dance to astronauts do?
The moon walk!

What is a frog's favorite game?
Hop scotch!

How did the frog feel when
she hurt her leg?
Un-hoppy!

Where do fish sleep?
In their river bed!

What do frogs eat on
really hot days?
Hop-sicles!

Why was the lamp sad at the beach?
He forgot to bring his shades!

What do you call a girl who
likes to cook outside?
Barbie!

Why did the mom serve
hay for dinner?
Her son could eat like a horse!

Why did the cow wear a bell on
the way to the farm?
Her horn didn't work!

What do you call the girl who
has a frog on her head?
Lily!

What do you get if you dive
into the Red Sea?
Wet!

Why did the dog make friends
with the tree?
He liked its bark!

How can you tell when a train is
eating its lunch?

It goes choo-choo!

How can you get rich by eating?

Just eat Fortune Cookies!

Why didn't the bird pay for dinner?

It was too cheep!

Where do monkeys do
their exercise?
The jungle gym!

Why didn't the moon finish its dinner?
It was full!

What sort of dog really
loves bubble baths?
Shampoodles!

Funnier
Knock Knock Jokes!

Knock knock.

Who's there?

Phil.

Phil who?

Phil the car please.
We're low on gas!

Knock knock.

Who's there?

Art.

Art who?

r2 d2!

Knock knock.

Who's there?

Annie.

Annie who?

Annie idea when this rain will stop? I'm getting wet!

Knock knock.

Who's there?

Chicken.

Chicken who?

I'm chicken under the mat and I can't find the key! Noooo!

Knock knock.

Who's there?

Waiter.

Waiter who?

Waiter I tell your mom!
You're in trouble now!

Knock knock.

Who's there?

Hijack.

Hijack who?

HiJack, is Jill home?

Knock knock.

Who's there?

Jester.

Jester who?

Jester minute!
Where's your doorbell?

Knock knock.

Who's there?

Wire.

Wire who?

Wire you still inside?
Let's go!

Knock knock.

Who's there?

Adam.

Adam who?

**If you Adam up I'll pay
half the bill!**

Knock knock.

Who's there?

Irish.

Irish who?

**Irish I was taller.
Then I could reach the doorbell!**

Knock knock.

Who's there?

Tommy.

Tommy who?

**My Tommy is too full!
I ate too much candy!
Noooo!**

Knock knock.

Who's there?

Lion.

Lion who?

**Lion down because
I'm really tired.
Goodnight!**

Knock knock.

Who's there?

Flea.

Flea who?

I knocked Flea times!
Why didn't you answer?

Knock knock.

Who's there?

Goose.

Goose who?

Goose who is here for dinner?
Uncle Bob!

Knock knock.

Who's there?

Dwayne.

Dwayne who?

**Dwayne the pool quickly!
I think Billy fell in!**

Knock knock.

Who's there?

Teresa.

Teresa who?

**Teresa very green this
time of year!**

Knock knock.

Who's there?

Mint.

Mint who?

**I mint to tell you.
Your doorbell is broken!
Ha! Ha!**

Knock knock.

Who's there?

Lava.

Lava who?

I Lava you so much!

Knock knock.

Who's there?

Robin.

Robin who?

Robin you!
Hands up and fill my
bag with money!

Knock knock.

Who's there?

Emma.

Emma who?

Emma very hungry!
What's for lunch?

Knock knock.

Who's there?

Wendy.

Wendy who?

Wendy doorbell works, please let me know!

Knock knock.

Who's there?

Kanye.

Kanye who?

Kanye please open this door before it starts to rain!

Knock knock.

Who's there?

Turnip.

Turnip who?

Turnip the music!
It's time to party!

Knock knock.

Who's there?

Hippo.

Hippo who?

Hippo birthday to you!
Hippo birthday to you!

Knock knock.

Who's there?

Bacon.

Bacon who?

I'm bacon a cake for your birthday! Yummy!

Knock knock.

Who's there?

Eddy.

Eddy who?

Eddy body home? I ran out of food!

Laugh Out Loud
Q & A Jokes!

Which superhero has a part time
job pressing shirts?

Iron Man!

Why did the skeleton fail the test?

He was a numbskull!

How did the banana leave work early?

He split!

What do puppies eat at the movies?
Pupcorn!

Why are fish really clever?
They live in schools!

Why did the pirate get his
new ship so cheaply?
It was on sail!

What did the fairy use to
clean her teeth?
Fairy Floss!

Why did the toilet go to hospital?
It was feeling flushed!

Who is the boss of the bird bank?
The Ost-rich!

What do you hear if you cross
Bambi with a ghost?
Bamboooo!

What did the lazy dog do for fun?
Chase a parked car!

What do you call a very rich elf?
Welfy!

Why did the boy curl up
in the fireplace?
He wanted to sleep like a log!

Why did the policeman
arrest the cat?
He saw the kitty litter!

What did the puppy say when he
sat on sandpaper?
Ruff!

What kind of dog can tell the time?
A watch dog!

What is a small dog's favorite
type of pizza?
Pupparoni!

What do you call a bee that
complains all day?
A grumble bee!

What do you call a teddy that
makes coffee?
A bear-ista!

Why did the chicken join the band?
She already had the drumsticks!

What did the bee say when he
got home from work?
Honey, I'm home!

What is a cat's favorite color?
PURRRRR_ple!

How do you get a spaceman's baby to sleep?
Rocket!

What did the duck say when it was his turn to pay?
Just put it on my bill!

What is the worst type of
jam in the world?

A traffic jam!

What did the elephant wear
in the pool?

Swimming trunks!

Why did the strawberry look so sad?

It was a blue berry!

Why did Santa call his dog 'Frost'?
Frost bites!

What did the policeman
say to the robber snowman?
Freeze!

Why don't starfish take a bath?
They wash up on the shore!

What are 2 birds in love called?
Tweet hearts!

Why did the dustpan
marry the broom?
She was swept off her feet!

What is the quietest dog
in the world?
A hush puppy!

What did one snowman
say to the other?
Can you smell carrots?

What did the potato chip
say to the biscuit?
Let's go for a dip!

Why did the lady wear a
helmet to dinner?
She was on a crash diet!

Why did the computer let out
a tiny squeak?

Someone stepped on its mouse!

What sort of music do
frogs listen to?

Hip Hop!

Where do whales get fast food?

The dive through!

Crazy Knock Knock Jokes!

Knock knock.

Who's there?

Justin.

Justin who?

Justin time for dinner!
Smells good!

Knock knock.

Who's there?

Ice cream.

Ice cream who?

Ice cream when I
jump in the pool!
It's fun!

Knock knock.

Who's there?

Who Who.

Who Who Who?

**How long have you
had a pet owl?**

Knock knock.

Who's there?

Icing.

Icing who?

**Icing many songs.
Would you like to hear one?**

Knock knock.

Who's there?

Ben.

Ben who?

Ben knocking so long I forgot why I'm here!

Knock knock.

Who's there?

Zany.

Zany who?

Zany body home today? Let me in!

Knock knock.

Who's there?

Soda.

Soda who?

Soda you want to let me in or what?

Knock knock.

Who's there?

Iran.

Iran who?

Iran really fast to get here and you're not even ready!

Knock knock.

Who's there?

Taco.

Taco who?

I want to Taco bout why your bell doesn't work!

Knock knock.

Who's there?

Wayne.

Wayne who?

**Wayne is coming!
I'm getting wet!
Noooo!**

Knock knock.

Who's there?

Amanda.

Amanda who?

Amanda repair that window you broke wants to charge me $200!

Knock knock.

Who's there?

Mikey.

Mikey who?

Mikey is too big for the keyhole! Noooooo!

Knock knock.

Who's there?

Vitamin.

Vitamin who?

Vitamin for the party!
He's a lot of fun!

Knock knock.

Who's there?

Renata.

Renata who?

Renata sugar!
Do you have any?

Knock knock.

Who's there?

Zookeeper.

Zookeeper who?

**Zookeeper way from Bobby!
He's got measles!**

Knock knock.

Who's there?

Omar.

Omar who?

**Omar goodness!
I love your shirt!
Where did you get it?**

Knock knock.

Who's there?

Honey bee.

Honey bee who?

Honey bee kind and open the door for your grandma!

Knock knock.

Who's there?

Wanda.

Wanda who?

I Wanda what Billy's up to today? Let's go ask him!

Knock knock.

Who's there?

Obi wan.

Obi wan who?

**Obi Wan of your best friends!
Let me in!**

Knock knock.

Who's there?

Abby.

Abby who?

**Abby new year!
Let's celebrate!**

Knock knock.

Who's there?

Utah.

Utah who?

**Utah one who asked me over!
Remember?**

Knock knock.

Who's there?

Izzy.

Izzy who?

**Izzy doorbell working yet?
It's been 2 years!**

Knock knock.

Who's there?

Elsa.

Elsa who?

**Who Elsa do you think
it would be?
Let me in!**

Knock knock.

Who's there?

Boo.

Boo who?

**Don't cry so much,
it's only a joke!**

Knock knock.

Who's there?

Tank.

Tank who?

You're very welcome sir!

Knock knock.

Who's there?

Icy.

Icy who?

**Icy you had a haircut.
It looks great!**

What kind of key will never
unlock a door?
A mon-key!

How did the barber win the marathon?
He took a shortcut!

What do you call a wizard
crossed with a pony?
Harry Trotter!

How did the pig write a letter?
With his pig pen!

What did the cute little
girl fish play with?
Doll-fins!

Why did the golfer go to the dentist?
She got a hole in one!

What did the dad bee
say to his kids?
Beehive yourself!

Why did the cow yell at the sheep?
She was in a bad MOOO-d!

What do crabs do on their birthday?
They shell-abrate!

What do you call a ketchup bottle in space?

A flying saucer!

How did the plumber get to school?

On the tool bus!

What did the cow say on January the 1st?

Happy Moo Year!

How did the snail get
across the lake?
In her snail-boat!

Where did the T-Rex buy
a birthday gift?
The dino-store!

Why did the biscuit go to the doctor?
He was feeling crummy!

What did the big wall say
to the smaller wall?

Let's catch up at the corner!

What did the baby corn
ask his mother?

Where is pop corn?

Why did the chicken
cross the playground?

To get to the other slide!

Why wouldn't the oyster
share her pearls?
She was a little shellfish!

Why was the beach wet?
The sea weed!

When is the best time
to buy a bird?
When they are going cheep!

What do puppies eat to
grow faster?
Fur-tilizer!

Why was the cat really
scared of the tree?
Because of its bark!

Why did the frog go to hospital?
To get a hopperation!

What side of a bird has
the most feathers?
The outside!

Where did the turtle stop
to get a snack?
The shell station!

Why did the boy run around
and around his bed 4 times?
To catch up on some sleep!

What time do ducks wake up?
The quack of dawn!

How did the artist keep clean?
He drew a bath!

How did the sun say
hi to the clouds?
With a heat wave!

Why was the computer feeling old?
It was losing its memory!

What do you call a fly that has lost its wings?
A walk!

Why did the chicken go for a jog?
She needed the egg-cersize

Silly Knock Knock Jokes!

Knock knock.

Who's there?

Witches.

Witches who?

Witches the fastest way to my house from here?

Knock knock.

Who's there?

Heaven.

Heaven who?

Heaven seen you in ages! You're looking good!

Knock knock.

Who's there?

Carrie.

Carrie who?

Can you Carrie my bag for me?
Thank you so much!

Knock knock.

Who's there?

Ears.

Ears who?

Ears another funny joke!
Ha Ha!

Knock knock.

Who's there?

Wilma.

Wilma who?

**Wilma key ever work
on this door?
Can I get a new one?**

Knock knock.

Who's there?

Iva.

Iva who?

**Iva very sore hand from
all this knocking!**

Knock knock.

Who's there?

Alby.

Alby who?

Alby back in a minute, so just wait there please!

Knock knock.

Who's there?

Stew.

Stew who?

**Stew early to go home!
Let's go to the park!**

Knock knock.

Who's there?

Greta.

Greta who?

**Greta move on!
We have to go!**

Knock knock.

Who's there?

Arthur.

Arthur who?

**Arthur any leftovers from lunch?
I'm really hungry!**

Knock knock.

Who's there?

Voodoo.

Voodoo who?

Voodoo you think it is knocking?
Santa Claus?

Knock knock.

Who's there?

CD.

CD who?

CD car out the front?
That's my new car!
Woo Hoo!

Knock knock.

Who's there?

Candy.

Candy who?

Candy door be answered faster next time please?

Knock knock.

Who's there?

Sister.

Sister who?

Sister right place for the party tonight? Turn up the music!

Knock knock.

Who's there?

Thor.

Thor who?

My hand is Thor from all this knocking!

Knock knock.

Who's there?

Lego.

Lego who?

Lego of the handle so I can open this door!

Knock knock.

Who's there?

Luke.

Luke who?

**Luke through the window
and find out!**

Knock knock.

Who's there?

Randy.

Randy who?

**Randy whole way from
my house!
Let's play ball!**

Knock knock.

Who's there?

Colin.

Colin who?

Colin all cars! Colin all cars! Emergency!

Knock knock.

Who's there?

Barbie.

Barbie who?

Barbie Q Chicken for dinner? Yummy!

Knock knock.

Who's there?

Summer.

Summer who?

Summer my friends like funny jokes. How about you?

Knock knock.

Who's there?

Needle.

Needle who?

Needle hand to move your TV? I've got big muscles!

Knock knock.

Who's there?

Lefty.

Lefty who?

Lefty key at home so I had to knock!

Knock knock.

Who's there?

Noah.

Noah who?

Noah good place for lunch? How about pizza?

Knock knock.

Who's there?

Des.

Des who?

**Des no way I can reach the bell!
Help!**

Knock knock.

Who's there?

Window.

Window who?

**Window we start holidays?
I think it's next week!
Yay!**

Bonus
Q & A Jokes!

What exercise do cats do
in the morning?
Puss Ups!

What was in the scary ghost's nose?
Boooogers!

What is a sailor's favorite lunch?
Fish and ships!

What was the witch's favorite subject at witch school?

Spelling!

Why was the wall cold?

He needed another coat of paint!

Who brought Christmas presents to baby sharks?

Santa Jaws!

Why did the vampire have to go
to the hospital?
He was coffin!

Why was the martial arts expert
in bed?
He had the kung flu!

Why did the computer wear glasses?
To improve it's web sight!

Why did the fireman ring in sick?
He was feeling burned out!

Where did the mouse park
his row boat?
The hickory dickory dock!

What is a skunks favorite
Christmas song?
Jingle smells, jingle smells!

What do fish like to watch on TV?

Whale of Fortune!

Why do bakers go to banks?

To get more dough!

What is a superhero's
favorite cereal?

Iron Bran!

What is a chicken's
favorite vegetable?
Broc, broc, broc, broccoli!

Why did the scarecrow get a
big pay rise?
He was a leader in his field!

What did the nose say to the finger?
Quit picking on me!

What did one egg say to
the other?

Eggs-cuse me, please!

Why is the ocean always so clean?

Mermaids!

Why are pirates pirates?

Because they ARRRRRRRRRR!!

Where do cows go on their day off?
The Mooseum!

What do you hear after 2 porcupines have a kiss?
Ouch!

Where did the really cool mouse live?
In his mousepad!

What do snakes do after
an argument?
Hiss and make up!

What do you call the bunny that
comes 3 days after Easter?
Choco Late!

Why are baby cows so cute?
They are adora-bull!

What kind of dog did the ghost have?
A booo-dle!

What sort of music do planets
love to sing?
Neptunes!

Why did the banana end up
in hospital?
It wasn't peeling very well!

What do you call a snake that has no clothes on?

Snaked!

Why did the boy stand on a cow?

To be a cowboy!

What did the taxi driver say to the frog?

Hop in!

How do monsters keep their hair so neat?

With scare spray!

Why did the baker keep on baking and baking?

She was on a roll!

Why didn't the girl like the pizza joke?

It was way too cheesy!

What has 40 legs but can't walk?
Half a centipede!

Why did the computer go crazy?
It had a screw loose!

How do fleas get to the next town?
They catch a dog!

Bonus Knock Knock Jokes!

Knock knock.

Who's there?

Pasta.

Pasta who?

**It's Pasta your bedtime!
Quick! Into bed!**

Knock knock.

Who's there?

Freddy.

Freddy who?

Freddy or not, here I come!

Knock knock.

Who's there?

Sarah.

Sarah who?

Is Sarah another way we can open this door?

Knock knock.

Who's there?

Lettuce.

Lettuce who?

Lettuce in please. We are really tired!

Knock knock.

Who's there?

Funnel.

Funnel who?

Funnel start in just a minute! Woohoo!

Knock knock.

Who's there?

Athena.

Athena who?

Athena bear in your house so RUN!!!!!

Knock knock.

Who's there?

Juicy.

Juicy who?

Juicy the news!
Our team won!
Yayyy!

Knock knock.

Who's there?

Kent.

Kent who?

Kent you see I like candy!
Can I eat yours?

Knock knock.

Who's there?

Cupid.

Cupid who?

Cupid quiet please!
I'm trying to sleep here!

Knock knock.

Who's there?

Anita.

Anita who?

Anita new key for this door!
Do you have one?

Knock knock.

Who's there?

Betty.

Betty who?

Betty you can't guess how many times I have knocked on this door? 27 times!

Knock knock.

Who's there?

West.

West who?

If you need a West from eating your lunch I can eat it for you!

Knock knock.

Who's there?

Stella.

Stella who?

**Let's Stella 'nother joke!
Ha! Ha!**

Knock knock.

Who's there?

Frank.

Frank who?

**Frank you very much for finally
opening this door!**

Knock knock.

Who's there?

Harry.

Harry who?

**Harry up!
I need to pee!**

Knock knock.

Who's there?

Carla.

Carla who?

**Can you Carla taxi for me
please? Thank you so much!**

Knock knock.

Who's there?

Yah.

Yah who?

Yahoo!
Ride 'em cowboy!

Knock knock.

Who's there?

Donna.

Donna who?

Donna want to make a big
deal about it but your
doorbell is broken!

Knock knock.

Who's there?

Troy.

Troy who?

Troy to answer quicker next time please!

Knock knock.

Who's there?

Dishes.

Dishes who?

Dishes the police! Open up!

Knock knock.

Who's there?

Alaska.

Alaska who?

**Alaska you one more time!
Please open the door!**

Knock knock.

Who's there?

Howard.

Howard who?

**Howard you like to go to the
park and play ball?**

Knock knock.

Who's there?

Fiddle.

Fiddle who?

Fiddle make you happy I'll keep on telling jokes!

Knock knock.

Who's there?

Dozen.

Dozen who?

Dozen anybody want to let me in? It's cold out here!

Thank you!

.... so much for reading our book.

We hope you had lots of laughs and enjoyed these funny jokes.

We would appreciate it so much if you could leave us a review on Amazon. Reviews make a big difference and we appreciate your support. Thank you!

Our Joke Books are available as a series for all ages from 6-12.

To see our range of books or leave a review anytime please go to FreddyFrost.com.

Thanks again!

Freddy Frost

Made in the USA
Las Vegas, NV
10 September 2022

55059106R00061